WAJ

*For Mimi – without whose
ghosting this story would
only be half as spooky*

# GUMDROP
# FINDS A GHOST

*Story and pictures by Val Biro*

HODDER AND STOUGHTON
LONDON SYDNEY AUCKLAND TORONTO

ON A SUNNY MORNING in June, Mr Josiah Oldcastle twitched his floppy moustache. 'Dan,' he said to his grandson, 'let's go out today and visit Mildew Manor, the ancestral home of Sir Marmaduke Ricketty-Cobwebb. It is a very old house and who knows, we might even meet a ghost!'

PR 6719

Dan was not so sure about meeting ghosts because they were
apt to shuffle and moan around in a most alarming way. But
when he saw the bulging picnic basket he was glad; and when
he heard that they would go in Gumdrop, he was delighted.
He jumped into the car and announced: 'I'm ready – let's go!'

Mildew Manor was an awesome sight.
You would have expected a ghost – a veritable
host of ghosts – to appear out of its nooks and crannies
at any moment. Dan felt a little scared at the thought.

'Don't worry,' said Mr Oldcastle,
'just hold my hand as we go round the
house. If we do meet a ghost, I shall
twitch my moustache and frighten it
off.' So they parked Gumdrop in a safe
place and joined the other visitors to
the Manor.

They walked through the hall and Dan thought that the fierce-looking suits of armour might leap into life at any moment and chase all the visitors away. But they remained motionless.

In the drawing room they saw a vast fireplace and Dan thought that a ghost might slide down the chimney and begin to shuffle and moan. But there was not a sound.

They went into the State Bedroom, and Dan half expected to see a ghost stretched out in the huge four-poster. But the bed was empty.

In the Picture Gallery hung the portraits of all the Ricketty-Cobwebbs. One of them, Sir Crankshaft, had apparently been very fond of cars, but he was a bad driver and very forgetful. He went for a drive on the Estate one day and walked back without his car. He said that he had lost it – but he had forgotten where!

'Fancy losing a car!' thought Dan. Sir Crankshaft must have been a very odd old man indeed.

It was when they walked along a dark and shadowy passage that it happened. To their horror, they saw a swaying, shuffling, wavering figure gliding towards them. A ghost! It uttered strange moans and everybody shrieked and ran away as fast as they could. Dan wanted to run too. But Mr Oldcastle stood firm. He twitched his moustache. Once. Twice. Three times.

And a funny thing happened. The ghost stopped moaning and began to giggle. Then it burst into laughter, took its head off and tucked it under its arm. Its real head was still laughing. 'Foiled again!' laughed the ghost. 'If I may say so, your moustache is so amusing that I can't keep this up any longer. Allow me to introduce myself – I am Sir Marmaduke Ricketty-Cobwebb, owner of this Manor.'

Dan was greatly relieved to see that it was not a real ghost after all. 'My visitors really do want to see a ghost,' explained Sir Marmaduke as he escorted them out of the house. 'Unfortunately we haven't got one, so I have to pretend to be one myself. But it is rather wearisome to go shuffling and moaning around all day, just to keep the visitors happy. Now, if only I could find a *real* ghost, I would have a special room set aside for it with a notice saying *This Way to The Ghost*.'

They had reached the car park by now, and when Sir Marmaduke saw Gumdrop he jumped about as if *he* had seen a ghost. 'What a beautiful car!' he exclaimed. 'How my uncle Crankshaft would have loved it! How I wish that *I* owned a lovely old car like this!' Mr Oldcastle understood the feeling and suggested that Sir Marmaduke come with them in Gumdrop and share their picnic.

They drove off across the Estate and up a steep track towards a wood on top of the hill. 'This is a lovely spot,' said Sir Marmaduke, 'I haven't been here for years. Let's have our picnic.' So they stopped Gumdrop, spread a rug on the grass, and settled down. Dan climbed into Gumdrop's driving seat – his very favourite place.

After the picnic Sir Marmaduke got up. 'Do you mind if I do a spot of ghost-practising? I still have a lot to learn — not least to refrain from laughing when people twitch their moustaches at me.' So saying, he started to shuffle and glide around, uttering his strange moans — while Mr Oldcastle twitched his floppy moustache at him.

Dan found all this so
funny that he laughed and
jumped up and down in the
driving seat. In doing so he must have
kicked against Gumdrop's handbrake, because slowly the car
started to move downhill!

'Stop, Dan, stop!' yelled Mr
Oldcastle. 'Pull the handbrake!
Press the footbrake!' Gumdrop was
rolling down the track quite fast
now and Dan grabbed the steering
wheel. His leg was too short to reach
the footbrake and he had no hand to spare for the
handbrake. It was hard work steering the runaway Gumdrop
on that steep track and as they reached a sharp bend, Dan was
quite unable to turn the wheel quickly enough.

So Gumdrop rolled straight on, across a ditch and down towards the edge of the Estate.

Dan steered Gumdrop between some trees and bushes which helped to slow him down. It wasn't downhill any more and, with a little *bump*, Gumdrop finally stopped. He was hardly visible among the foliage.

'Where have they got to?' called Sir Marmaduke anxiously.
'I've never seen this part of the Estate before!' They searched
for some time, when Mr Oldcastle discovered Gumdrop and
Dan in the bushes and was much relieved to find that neither
of them had come to much harm. 'Well done, my boy,' he
said, 'you will make a fine driver one day!'

Dan was much relieved too, although his legs were still shaking a bit. He pushed his way through the foliage to see what Gumdrop had bumped against. He looked – then he stared – and then he shouted excitedly. 'Come and look! See what Gumdrop has found! A great big leafy mouldy mildewy muddy beautiful old car!!'

Mr Oldcastle stared too and twitched his moustache so many times that his glasses fell off. Then he started shouting. 'This is a veritable Ghost! Sir Marmaduke, come and see a Ghost!'

It was Sir Marmaduke's turn to stare and shout now. 'This must be the car which my uncle Crankshaft lost all those years ago! And your clever Gumdrop has actually found it at last!' He jumped about for joy. 'But why did you call it a ghost?' he asked when he calmed down a bit. 'Because, my dear Sir,' replied Mr Oldcastle, 'this car is a Rolls-Royce Silver Ghost!'

And so it was that Gumdrop had found a ghost for Mildew Manor, and a lovely old car for Sir Marmaduke. It is on view to this day at the Manor, beautifully repaired and polished, in a room specially set aside for it, with a notice saying

THIS WAY TO
THE GHOST

**Rolls-Royce Silver Ghost
1909**

**LOST**
by Sir Crankshaft Ricketty-Cobwebb
**1911**
**FOUND**
last Summer on the Estate
by Gumdrop

People come for miles to see this *real* and lovely ghost, and Sir Marmaduke has no need to shuffle and moan around any more.

And on warm and sunny days he asks Mr Oldcastle and Dan to come over in Gumdrop and they drive round the Estate, Gumdrop in front, the Ghost behind, to the delight of all.

# Mildew Manor

Showing the Ancestral and
HAUNTED Home of Sir Marmaduke
Ricketty-Cobwebb, on the Day
of GUMDROP's Visit